D0908578

FAIRIES AND CHIMNEYS

By ROSE FYLEMAN

THE CHILD NEXT DOOR HAS A WREATH ON HER
   HAT.

HER AFTERNOON FROCK STICKS OUT LIKE THAT,
   ALL SOFT AND FRILLY;

FAIRIES AND CHIMNEYS

BY
ROSE FYLEMAN

GARDEN CITY   NEW YORK
DOUBLEDAY, DORAN & COMPANY, Inc.
1933

PRINTED IN THE UNITED STATES OF AMERICA

TO
THE *REALEST* FAIRY
OF MY CHILDHOOD

MY MOTHER

CONTENTS

I

FAIRIES AND CHIMNEYS

CONTENTS

II

BIRD LORE

[viii]

CONTENTS

FAIRIES AND CHIMNEYS

FAIRIES AND CHIMNEYS

FAIRIES

THERE are fairies at the bottom of our garden!
  It's not so very, very far away;
You pass the gardener's shed and you just keep
    straight ahead—
  I do so hope they've really come to stay.
There's a little wood, with moss in it and beetles,
  And a little stream that quietly runs through;
You wouldn't think they'd dare to come merry-
    making there—
      Well, they do.

There are fairies at the bottom of our garden!
  They often have a dance on summer nights;
The butterflies and bees make a lovely little breeze,
  And the rabbits stand about and hold the lights.

[13]

FAIRIES AND CHIMNEYS

FAIRIES [*Continued*]

Did you know that they could sit upon the moon-
beams
  And pick a little star to make a fan,
And dance away up there in the middle of the air?
  Well, they can.

There are fairies at the bottom of our garden!
  You cannot think how beautiful they are;
They all stand up and sing when the Fairy Queen
    and King
  Come gently floating down upon their car.
The King is very proud and *very* handsome;
  The Queen—now can you guess who that could
    be
(She's a little girl all day, but at night she steals
    away)?
          Well—it's ME!

YESTERDAY IN OXFORD STREET

YESTERDAY in Oxford Street, oh, what d'you think,
    my dears?
I had the most exciting time I've had for years and
    years;
The buildings looked so straight and tall, the sky
    was blue between,
And, riding on a motor-bus, I saw the fairy
    queen!

Sitting there upon the rail and bobbing up and
    down,
The sun was shining on her wings and on her golden
    crown;
And looking at the shops she was, the pretty silks
    and lace—
She seemed to think that Oxford Street was quite
    a lovely place.

YESTERDAY IN OXFORD STREET [*Continued*]

And once she turned and looked at me, and waved
    her little hand;
But I could only stare and stare—oh, would she
    understand?
I simply couldn't speak at all, I simply couldn't
    stir,
And all the rest of Oxford Street was just a shining
    blur.

Then suddenly she shook her wings—a bird had
    fluttered by—
And down into the street she looked and up into the
    sky;
And perching on the railing on a tiny fairy toe,
She flashed away so quickly that I hardly saw her
    go.

I never saw her any more, altho' I looked all day;
Perhaps she only came to peep, and never meant to
    stay:

    [16]

FAIRIES AND CHIMNEYS

YESTERDAY IN OXFORD STREET [*Continued*]

But oh, my dears, just think of it, just think what
    luck for me,
That she should come to Oxford Street, and I be
    there to see!

A FAIRY WENT A-MARKETING

A FAIRY went a-marketing—
   She bought a little fish;
She put it in a crystal bowl
   Upon a golden dish.
An hour she sat in wonderment
   And watched its silver gleam,
And then she gently took it up
   And slipped it in a stream.

A fairy went a-marketing—
   She bought a coloured bird;
It sang the sweetest, shrillest song
   That ever she had heard.
She sat beside its painted cage
   And listened half the day,
And then she opened wide the **door**
   And let it fly away.

[18]

A FAIRY WENT A-MARKETING [*Continued*]

A fairy went a-marketing—
 She bought a winter gown
All stitched about with gossamer
 And lined with thistledown.
She wore it all **the afternoon**
 With prancing and delight,
Then gave it to a little frog
 To keep him warm at night.

A fairy went a-marketing—
 She bought a gentle mouse
To take her tiny messages,
 To keep her tiny house.
All day she kept its busy feet
 Pit-patting to and fro,
And then she kissed its silken **ears,**
 Thanked it, and let it go.

I STOOD AGAINST THE WINDOW

I STOOD against the window
    And looked between the bars,
And there were strings of fairies
    Hanging from the stars;
Everywhere and everywhere
    In shining, swinging chains;
The air was full of shimmering,
    Like sunlight when it rains.

They kept on swinging, swinging,
    They flung themselves so high
They caught upon the pointed moon
    And hung across the sky.
And when I woke next morning,
    There still were crowds and crowds
In beautiful bright bunches
    All sleeping on the clouds.

[20]

THE FOUNTAIN

UPON the terrace where I play
A little fountain sings all day
    A tiny tune;
It leaps and prances in the air—
I saw a little fairy there
    This afternoon.

The jumping fountain never stops—
He sat upon the highest drops
    And bobbed about;
His legs were waving in the sun,
He seemed to think it splendid fun—
    I heard him shout.

The sparrows watched him from a tree,
A robin bustled up to see
    Along the path:
I thought my wishing-bone would break,
I wished so much that I could take
    A fairy bath.

THE BEST GAME THE FAIRIES PLAY

THE best game the fairies play,
  The best game of all,
Is sliding down steeples—
  (You know they're very tall).
You fly to the weathercock,
  And when you hear it crow
You fold your wings and clutch your things
  And then let go!

They have a million other games—
  Cloud-catching's one,
And mud-mixing after rain
  Is heaps and heaps of fun;
But when you go and stay with them
  Never mind the rest,
Take my advice—they're very nice,
  But steeple-sliding's best!

[22]

FAIRIES AND CHIMNEYS

HAVE YOU WATCHED THE FAIRIES?

Have you watched the fairies when the rain is done
Spreading out their little wings to dry them in the
sun?
I have, I have! Isn't it fun?

Have you heard the fairies all among the limes
Singing little fairy tunes to little fairy rhymes?
I have, I have, lots and lots of times!

Have you seen the fairies dancing in the air,
And dashing off behind the stars to tidy up their
hair?
I have, I have; I've been there!

THE CHILD NEXT DOOR

THE child next door has a wreath on her hat,
Her afternoon frock sticks out like that,
    All soft and frilly;
She doesn't believe in fairies at all
(She told me over the garden wall)—
    She thinks they're silly.

The child next door has a watch of her own,
She has shiny hair and her name is Joan
    (Mine's only Mary),
But doesn't it seem very sad to you
To think that she never her whole life through
    Has seen a fairy?

DIFFERENCES

Daddy goes a-riding in a motor painted grey,
He makes a lot of snorty noise before he gets away;
The fairies go a-riding when they wish to take their
ease,
The fairies go a-riding on the backs of bumble-
bees.

Daddy goes a-sailing in a jolly wooden boat,
He takes a lot of tackle and his very oldest coat;
The fairies go a-sailing, and I wonder they get
home,
The fairies go a-sailing on a little scrap of foam.

Daddy goes a-climbing with a knapsack and a
stick,
The rocks are very hard and steep, his boots are
very thick;

[25]

DIFFERENCES [*Continued*]

But the fairies go a-climbing (I've seen them there
  in crowds),
The fairies go a-climbing on the mountains in the
  clouds.

MOTHER

When mother comes each morning
　　She wears her oldest things,
She doesn't make a rustle,
　　She hasn't any rings;
She says, "Good-morning, chickies,
　　It's such a lovely day,
Let's go into the garden
　　And have a game of play!"

When mother comes at tea-time
　　Her dress goes shoo-shoo-shoo,
She always has a little bag,
　　Sometimes a sunshade too;
She says, "I am so hoping
　　There's something left for me;
Please hurry up, dear Nanna,
　　I'm dying for my tea."

[27]

MOTHER [*Continued*]

When mother comes at bed-time
　　Her evening dress she wears,
She tells us each a story
　　When we have said our prayers;
And if there is a party
　　She looks so shiny bright
It's like a lovely fairy
　　Dropped in to say good-night.

GROWN-UPS

Aunties know all about fairies,
Uncles know all about guns,
Mothers and fathers think all the day long
Of making their children happy and strong,
Even the littlest ones.

CAT'S CRADLE

ALTHOUGH it has a jolly name
Cat's cradle is a funny game—
I like to play it all the same.

It's easy when you first begin,
But when it goes all long and thin
I daren't put my fingers in.

If mother's anywhere about
We stand against the door and shout
Until she comes and helps us out.

Her fingers look so long and white,
Her rings are very sparkly bright,
She almost always gets it right.

VISITORS

WHEN I was very ill in bed
  The fairies came to visit me;
They danced and played around my head,
  Tho' other people couldn't see.

Across the end a railing goes
  With bars and balls and twisted rings,
And there they jiggled on their toes
  And did the wonderfullest things.

They balanced on the golden balls,
  They jumped about from bar to bar,
And then they fluttered to the walls
  Where coloured birds and flowers are.

I watched them darting in and out,
  I watched them gaily climb and cling,
While all the flowers moved about
  And all the birds began to sing.

[31]

VISITORS [*Continued*]

    And when it was no longer light
      I felt them up my pillows creep,
    And there they sat and sang all night—
      I heard them singing in my sleep.

WISHES

I wish I liked rice pudding,
I wish I were a twin,
I wish some day a real live fairy
Would just come walking in.

I wish when I'm at table
My feet would touch the floor,
I wish our pipes would burst next winter,
Just like they did next door.

I wish that I could whistle
Real proper grown-up tunes,
I wish they'd let me sweep the chimneys
On rainy afternoons.

I've got such heaps of wishes,
I've only said a few;
I wish that I could wake some morning
And find they'd all come true!

[33]

THE BALLOON MAN

HE always comes on market days,
  And holds balloons—a lovely bunch—
And in the market square he stays,
  And never seems to think of lunch.

They're red and purple, blue and green,
  And when it is a sunny day
Tho' carts and people get between
  You see them shining far away.

And some are big and some are small,
  All tied together with a string,
And if there is a wind at all
  They tug and tug like anything.

Some day perhaps he'll let them go
  And we shall see them sailing high,
And stand and watch them from below—
  They *would* look pretty in the sky!

I DON'T LIKE BEETLES

I DON'T like beetles, tho' I'm sure they're very good,
I don't like porridge, tho' my Nanna says I should;
I don't like the cistern in the attic where I play,
And the funny noise the bath makes when the water
    runs away.

I don't like the feeling when my gloves are made of
    silk,
And that dreadful slimy skinny stuff on top of hot
    milk;
I don't like tigers, not even in a book,
And, I know it's very naughty, but I don't like
    Cook!

VERY LOVELY

Wouldn't it be lovely if the rain came down
Till the water was quite high over all the town?
If the cabs and buses all were set afloat,
And we had to go to school in a little boat?

Wouldn't it be lovely if it still should pour
And we all went up to live on the second floor?
If we saw the butcher sailing up the hill,
And we took the letters in at the window sill?

It's been raining, raining, all the afternoon;
All these things might happen really very soon.
If we woke to-morrow and found they had begun,
Wouldn't it be glorious? *Wouldn't* it be fun?

SUMMER MORNING

THE air around was trembling-bright
And full of dancing specks of light,
While butterflies were dancing too
Between the shining green and blue.
I might not watch, I might not stay,
I ran along the meadow way.

The straggling brambles caught my feet,
The clover field was, oh! so sweet;
I heard a singing in the sky,
And busy things went buzzing by;
And how it came I cannot tell,
But all the hedges sang as well.

Along the clover-field I ran
To where the little wood began,

SUMMER MORNING [*Continued*]

And there I understood at last
Why I had come so far, so fast—
On every leaf of every tree
A fairy sat and smiled at me!

FAIRY SONG

Dance, little friend, little friend breeze,
Low among the hedgerows, high among the trees;
Fairy partners wait for you, oh, do not miss your
    chance,
        Dance, little friend, dance!

Sing, little friend, little friend stream,
Softly through the mossy nooks where fairies lie
    and dream;
Sweetly by the rushes where fairies sway and swing,
        Sing, little friend, sing!

Shine, little friend, little friend moon,
The fairies will have gathered in the forest very
    soon;
Send your gleaming silver darts where thick the
    branches twine,
        Shine, little friend, shine!

INVITATION

IF you will come and stay with us
  You shall not want for ease;
We'll swing you on a cobweb
  Between the forest trees.
And twenty little singing birds
  Upon a flowering thorn
Shall hush you every evening
  And wake you every morn.

If you will come and stay with us
  You need not miss your school,
A learned toad shall teach you,
  High-perched upon his stool.
And he will tell you many things
  That none but fairies know—
The way the wind goes wandering,
  And how the daisies grow.

INVITATION [*Continued*]

> If you will come and stay with us
>   You shall not lack, my dear,
> The finest fairy raiment,
>   The best of fairy cheer.
> We'll send a million glow-worms out,
>   And slender chains of light
> Shall make a shining pathway—
>   Then why not come to-night?

FAIRIES AND CHIMNEYS

You know the smoke from chimneys—
  It often isn't smoke,
It's nothing but the fairies
  Having such a joke.
Round they fly and round about,
  Higher still and higher—
"Dearie me," the people say,
  "A chimney on fire!"

You know the noise the wind makes
  At night-time now and then—
It's just those naughty fairies
  At their tricks again—
Sitting in the chimney
  Round and round in rows,
Singing all together
  And warming up their toes.

[42]

WHITE MAGIC

BLIND folk see the fairies,
　　Oh, better far than we,
Who miss the shining of their wings
Because our eyes are filled with things
　　We do not wish to see.
They need not seek enchantment
　　From solemn, printed books,
For all about them as they go
The fairies flutter to and fro
　　With smiling, friendly looks.

Deaf folk hear the fairies
　　However soft their song;
'Tis we who lose the honey sound
Amid the clamour all around
　　That beats the whole day long.

[43]

WHITE MAGIC [*Continued*]

But they with gentle faces
  Sit quietly apart;
What room have they for sorrowing
While fairy minstrels sit and sing
  Close to their listening heart?

FAIRIES AND CHIMNEYS

THERE USED TO BE——

THERE used to be fairies in Germany—
  I know, for I've seen them there
In a great cool wood where the tall trees stood
  With their heads high up in the air;
They scrambled about in the forest
  And nobody seemed to mind;
They were dear little things (tho' they didn't have
    wings)
  And they smiled and their eyes were kind.

What, and oh what were they doing
  To let things like this?
How could it be? And didn't they see
  That folk were going amiss?
Were they too busy playing,
  Or can they perhaps have slept,
That never they heard an ominous word
  That stealthily crept and crept?

THERE USED TO BE——[*Continued*]

There used to be fairies in Germany—
　The children will look for them still;
They will search all about till the sunlight slips
　　out
　And the trees stand frowning and chill.
"The flowers," they will say, "have all vanished,
　And where can the fairies be fled
That played in the fern?"—The flowers will re-
　　turn,
　But I fear that the fairies are dead.

FAIRIES AND CHIMNEYS

IF

If I were a bird with a dear little nest
  I should always be going for flights,
I'd fly to the North and the South and the West
  And see all the wonderful sights.
I'd perch on the point of the very tall spires,
  And race with the insects and bees,
And there would be parties on telegraph wires,
  And school at the top of the trees.

If I were a fairy and lived in a flower,
  What fun, oh, what fun it would be!
I'm certain I never should sleep for an hour,
  And I'd always have honey for tea;
And never a stocking or shoe would I wear,
  Nor ever a hat on my head,
And no one would tell me to tidy my hair,
  And no one would send me to bed.

[47]

IF [*Continued*]

If I were a duchess in satin and pearls,
  I'd curtsey like this and like this;
I'd graciously smile at the lords and the earls,
  And give them my fingers to kiss.
And mother should dress all in silver and pink,
  And daddy in silver and green,
And off we should go in a coach, only think,
  To live with the King and the Queen!

FAIRIES AND CHIMNEYS

THE FAIRIES HAVE NEVER A PENNY TO SPEND

THE fairies have never a penny to spend,
    They haven't a thing put by,
But theirs is the dower of bird and of flower
    And theirs are the earth and the sky.
And though you should live in a palace of gold
    Or sleep in a dried-up ditch,
You could never be poor as the fairies are,
        And never as rich.

Since ever and ever the world began
    They have danced like a ribbon of flame,
They have sung their song through the centuries
        long
    And yet it is never the same.
And though you be foolish or though you be wise,
    With hair of silver or gold,
You could never be young as the fairies are,
        And never as old.

[49]

BIRD LORE

PEACOCKS

PEACOCKS sweep the fairies' rooms;
They use their folded tails for brooms;
But fairy dust is brighter far
Than any mortal colours are;
And all about their tails it clings
In strange designs of rounds and rings;
And that is why they strut about
And proudly spread their feathers out.

FAIRIES AND CHIMNEYS

THE CUCKOO

THE cuckoo is a tell-tale,
  A mischief-making bird;
He flies to East, he flies to West
And whispers into every nest
  The wicked things he's heard;
He loves to spread his naughty lies,
He laughs about it as he flies;
"Cuckoo," he cries, "cuckoo, cuckoo,
  It's true, it's true."

And when the fairies catch him
  His busy wings they dock,
They shut him up for evermore
(He may not go beyond the door)
  Inside a wooden clock;
Inside a wooden clock he cowers
And has to tell the proper hours—
"Cuckoo," he cries, "cuckoo, cuckoo,
  It's true, it's true."

[54]

THE ROOKS

HIGH in the elm-trees sit the rooks,
Or flit about with busy looks
   And solemn, ceaseless caws.
Small wonder they are so intent,
They are the fairies' Parliament—
   They make the fairy laws.

They never seem to stop all day,
And you can hear from far away
   Their busy chatter-chat.
They work so very hard indeed
You'd wonder that the fairies need
   So many laws as that.

THE ROBIN

THE robin is the fairies' page;
  They keep him neatly dressed
For country service or for town
In dapper livery of brown
  And little scarlet vest.

On busy errands all day long
  He hurries to and fro
With watchful eyes and nimble wings—
There are not very many things.
  The robin doesn't know.

And he can tell you, if he will,
  The latest fairy news:
The quaint adventures of the King,
And whom the Queen is visiting,
  And where she gets her shoes.
[56]

THE ROBIN [*Continued*]

And lately, when the fairy Court
    Invited me to tea,
He stood behind the Royal Chair;
And here, I solemnly declare,
When he discovered I was there,
    That robin *winked* at me.

THE COCK

THE kindly cock is the fairies' friend,
He warns them when their revels must end;
He never forgets to give the word,
For the cock is a thoroughly punctual bird.

And since he grieves that he never can fly,
Like all the other birds, up in the sky,
The fairies put him now and again
High on a church for a weather-vane.

Little for sun or for rain he cares;
He turns about with the proudest airs
And chuckles with joy as the clouds go past
To think he is up in the sky at last.

THE GROUSE

THE grouse that lives on the moorland wide
Is filled with a most ridiculous pride;
He thinks that it all belongs to him
And every one else must obey his whim.
When the queer wee folk who live on the moors
Come joyfully leaping out of their doors
To frisk about on the warm sweet heather
Laughing and chattering all together,
He looks askance at their rollicking play
And calls to them in the angriest way:
"You're a feather-brained, foolish, frivolous pack,
Go back, you rascally imps, go back!"

But little enough they heed his shout;
Over the rocks they tumble about;
They chase each other over the ling;
They kick their heels in the heather and sing;

THE GROUSE [*Continued*]

"Oho, Mr. Grouse, you'd best beware
Or some fine day, if you don't take care,
The witch who lives in the big brown bog
With a wise old weasel, a rat and a frog,
Will come a-capering over the fell
And put you under a horrible spell;
Your feathers will moult and your voice will crack—
Go back, you silly old bird, go back!"

THE SKYLARK

Of all the birds the fairies love the skylark much
    the best;
They come with little fairy gifts to seek his hidden
    nest;
They praise his tiny slender feet and silken suit
    of brown,
And with their gentle hands they smooth his
    feathers softly down.

They cluster round with glowing cheeks and bright
    expectant eyes,
Waiting the moment that shall bring the freedom
    of the skies;
Waiting the double-sweet delight that only he can
    give,
(Oh, kings might surely spurn their crowns to live
    as fairies live).

[61]

THE SKYLARK [*Continued*]

To ride upon a skylark's back between his happy
   wings,

To float upon the edge of heaven and listen while
   he sings—

The dreams of mortals scarce can touch so perfected
   a bliss,

And even fairies cannot know a greater joy than
   this.

1510   173   14